DONBRIDGE:

The Ring of Lazarus

~~~

RD Vincent
~~~

Note: If you purchased this book without a cover or received a copied version you should be aware that the content you are reading is stolen property.

DONBRIDGE: THE RING OF LAZARUS

ISBN: 9781515134848

Printed in the United States of America

For Grandma and Aunt Dorothy, your stories will live forever.

Acknowledgements

A special thanks to my editor, Faye Walker. Without your dedication to this series, it would not be possible. Thank you!

Grandmother stood at the gold-flecked formica countertop, chopping onions and then scraping them across the old cutting board, adding the pieces to the contents of a giant cast-iron pot. The pot had been bubbling a long time, probably since before her daughter had dropped the three grandchildren off on the way to the diner. In their world, overnight snowfall meant the joy of closed school, but for her it simply meant a longer drive to her job as a waitress

with a detour to stash the children at grandparents' house for the day.

"I don't like chili!" Jasper hissed behind Grandmamma's back. "She makes us eat it every time!"

"That's because it's cold out, silly," Michael shot back, defending his saintly grandmother.

"Then why is it called 'chilly?' Huh? If it's so cold, we should be eating 'warmy!'" Jasper stuck out his tongue and it took all Michael's strength not to knock him backwards in his chair.

Grandmamma already had to break up a fight between the boys over who got to pour the cereal, and she'd spent half an hour getting chewing gum out of little Mary's hair. Mary had howled like she was being ripped bald-headed. Michael didn't think Grandmamma could take much more.

"You'll eat it if you know what's good for you," Michael whispered, shoving his balled up fist against his palm.

"But Michael! She puts weird stuff in it!" Jasper whimpered, looking towards the stove. Michael made a face at him and took a menacing step in his direction, but Jasper countered by protesting, "I saw her! She put some brown stuff in it!"

"That's the peanut butter," Grandmamma said without turning around. Both boys jumped. "I've always put peanut butter in my chili."

"Really?" Michael asked, struggling to remember if he'd ever tasted it in all the years she'd been warming them up with her special snow day chili. "Why would you do that?"

"Well, it's all we had for a while when I was a girl back in Donbridge. It came in tins stamped 'non-perishable' on the side. It kept us

alive and strong when meat was scarce, especially during the war."

"Where's Donbridge?" Jasper asked quietly. Grandmamma lay her wooden spoon on the stove and walked to the dinette table, wiping her hands on her apron. She smiled and looked out the window to where the snow was still falling in giant puffs.

"I'll tell you all about it while you work," she said. She produced a bowl of potatoes and two rattly metal peelers from the counter. She sat, pulled up a bowl of carrots and a knife for herself and began to peel as she talked.

In the land surrounding the fertile Hudson valley, there was once a small town called Donbridge. The town was prosperous, and its history was filled with tales of miracles and wonder. Many believed the town's prosperity came from the days when the Lenape clans had resided there, and one local legend told of a Meteinu who had consecrated the valley by burying ohta dolls around its perimeter. The dolls offered protection against evil, and they were said to bring good fortune and health to his people.

The Lenape clans moved westward with the arrival of the Dutch in 1630, and by 1700 the English had settled across the Hudson Valley. A young English merchant named William Donbridge established a town and brought his new bride, Emma Starling. Far too young, Emma was the first resident to die in the newly christened town of Donbridge, and she was buried atop a hill overlooking the town.

Over time, more families settled in Donbridge, and their stories interwove with the Lenape legends. Some families were especially blessed with good fortune and good crops while others seemed to be cursed with only misfortune. One family, the Taylors who farmed grain on the western edge of Donbridge, were said to be doubly cursed.

Their daughter, Julianne, was an only child on the day she set out for a schoolmate's house, but that had not always been the case. The harsh hand of Fate had touched her young brother when he was only six months old. The loss of their second child was an unspoken pain her parents were never able to put aside. When the doctor had declared the young boy dead after a few days of raging fever, his mother, Mary Ann, had walked off the farm, returning three days later with no explanation. The heart of his father, Timothy, had died the day his little boy did.

In Julianne's tenth year, Donbridge experienced a sudden early autumn. The brisk air and the sky scattered with orange, yellow, and red as the leaves swirled put joy in Julianne's heart. Across the valley, rye and clover turned brown, and meadow mice scurried about the harvested straw grass fields, making off with the remnants to build their warm nests against the coming winter winds. Perched high above the fields in the nearly-bare branches of swamp maples, barn swallows roosted and squawked in harmony. Their songs and whistles summoned orchard orioles and fox sparrows. The beating wings and birdsong would go on for hours before the ruckus ended as if silenced by a greater power. The birds then took to the sky by the thousands, creating a thick black cloud as they began their migration to warmer places in the south.

The first week of October, Donbridge endured its first crippling, freezing rain, a stab in the weather which lasted into the early morning. Holsteins stood in the bogged pasture chewing their cuds while their black and white hides glossed over with frozen water droplets. The brown-green-orange fields and trees slowly glazed with ice, making all the world like glass. Icicles hung dripping from roof tops and bare branches, and every so often, the silence was punctuated by the gun shot of a branch exploding under the weight of so much ice, the water trapped inside its veins expanding more than the thin wood could hold. The weight of the ice pulled evergreen branches and weeping willow bands to the ground, creating archways and caves along the foot paths.

The first gray fingers of light crested the Steerage Mountain range when Julianne suddenly awoke to the heavy sound of rain against the slate roof. It took her a few moments to figure out she slept at the Sutton Cottage and the bundle snoring softly in the trundle bed nearby was her school friend, Amelia Sutton.

The Suttons' cottage lay in the far corner of the town and nearly an hour's walk from Julianne's farm. The Suttons were a quiet family who kept to themselves except when they were working. John Sutton was a leather currier and worked for Mr. Robert Sharp, who owned the leather tanning and textile factory. Sarah Sutton was the midwife of Donbridge and a healer due to her great knowledge and experience with herbs. Many people looked to her for medicine and relief beyond that which the village doctor could provide.

After a breakfast of fresh blackberry scones and tea in the Suttons' tiny fireside kitchen, Julianne prepared to head for home with the herbs her mother had sent her for. The girl gathered her satchel and hooded cape, and Mrs. Sutton handed her the packets and bottles of linseed oil, rosin, lampblack, and peppermint leaves. Julianne hugged Amelia and headed to the woods.

"What?" Jasper cried out, causing Michael to jump. He elbowed Jasper sharply, but Jasper only shoved back. He whined, "I'm not even allowed to go fetch the mail from the mailbox, and a girl her age is allowed to walk all the way home by herself? It's not fair!"

"Hmm, fair it might not be," Grandmamma agreed, patting his head and smiling. "But as you'll see, there's a reason why little children don't go walking in the woods on their own. Your mother's wise to keep you in the yard, lest the Panderlaub come after you."

"What's a Panderlaub?" Michael asked before Jasper could interrupt again.

Grandmamma looked around the room, and then craned her neck to make sure Mary was out of earshot. “I’ll tell you, but you have to promise me… no nightmares.”

The boys nodded their heads solemnly and Grandmamma returned to her task for a long, silent moment, weighing whether or not they were too young to hear. Finally, she took a deep breath and continued.

As Julianne walked along the wooded path cutting through the forest, a doe watched her cautiously, following her with its eyes for a moment from the safety of the thicket. Her tiny hooves smashed the frozen orchard grasses into shards as she walked, scattering the tiny ice crystals before her. Julianne startled at the flash of brown movement close by but ignored the doe as she felt a far more disturbing presence watching her from the trees. She trod the icy slush path, willing her feet to tread silently as her breath made a thick fog in the air.

The girl and the deer nearly crossed paths, but a sudden movement caused the doe to twitch its ears and freeze. Julianne lifted her small hands slowly to remove her cowl, and the deer darted off toward the end of the forest, snorting in fear. The girl turned her head, startled by the sound as the deer smashed ice all through the woods. The sound echoed until Julianne heard no more.

“Is someone there?” she called, turning in a rapid circle to peer into the shadows surrounding her. “Hello? Speak if you’re there, and make yourself known!”

Julianne looked about the forest, pushing aside her chestnut hair when a light breeze blew it around her face. Her wind burned skin shone like strawberry flecks. Her sapphire eyes darted wildly about and, seeing nothing of concern, she slowly placed her hood over her head and continued.

As the frozen ice crackled beneath Julianne's feet, she slipped forward over a patch that did not give way. Her foot rushed out in front of her, knocking her down. As she fell, she struck her knee against shale and the skin burst open. Rattled and nervous, she thought she'd broken her mother's herb bottles in the satchel. She carefully opened the bag and smiled when she saw the herbs were not damaged.

She stood. Suddenly, something shoved her from behind and sent her sprawling. Her head hit a jagged piece of shale, gouging her skin to the bone; while the impact left her dazed, numb from pain and disorientcd, the broken skin unleashed a torrent of blood that soon formed a halo around her head. As her eyes shut, a darkened figure stood over her, gazing at her still body which seemed smaller in death. The figure loosed a sigh of longing. Then it disappeared into the woods.

"Is she...dead, Grandmamma?" Jasper asked in a thin voice. Michael remembered he really wasn't all that big. He couldn't even be cross with Jasper for interrupting because he looked afraid. And because Michael wanted to know the answer himself.

"It would seem so, wouldn't it?" Grandmamma answered with a smile, except it was a smile that didn't touch her eyes.

"Who would do something like that to a little girl?" asked Jasper. The look of total betrayal on his face was heartbreaking. Even though Michael and Jasper usually fought, Michael felt the urge to slide his chair next to Jasper's and put his arm around the younger boy's shoulders.

"That's the mystery of it all," she answered. She shrugged her shoulders slightly in a way that suggested she might not ever tell. "Some say it was the Panderlaub that got her. But listen to what happened next."

Night reached across Donbridge. The wind blew the bare tree branches, scattering the leaves on the forest floor. It wasn't long before Julianne's body was covered by debris, hiding her amidst the surroundings.

In town, Old Man Keating was inching his way down the main street through the village, lighting the lamps. In the distance, he saw Timothy Taylor, Julianne's father, walking towards the center of town, leading his horse.

"Is something wrong, Timothy?" Mr. Keating asked as he lit another lantern.

"My daughter, Julianne... have you seen her?"

"Not since yesterday morning when she set out to the Sutton place... did she not come home?"

"No, we haven't heard from her," Mr. Taylor said. Old Man Keating heard the fear in Timothy's voice.

"Best if we get the sheriff; he'll know what to do." Keating saddled his horse and the two men headed toward the bass pond where Sheriff Jonathan Brine lived, a quarter mile outside town. A sheriff normally remained at the jail unless he could get a deputy to stay, but since prisoners were few and far between in Donbridge, Sheriff Brine spent his nights at home.

The moon shone brightly over the landscape as Old Man Keating and

Mr. Taylor rode swiftly through the forest. Sheriff Brine had finished his dinner and sat on the porch in a chair he'd fashioned from a pine tree fallen on his property in the last big storm. He leaned back against the outer wall of his log cabin, the occasional wisp of cigar smoke puffing gently around his head, reaching for the porch rafters. His face was covered in a full beard and he wore his hair long, almost over his eyes, so he looked more like a black bear than a man. Yet his eyes were deep brown, giving him a look both mellow and approachable. He rested his booted feet on the porch rail, staring at the great field beyond.

The sheriff leaned forward and stood at the sight of two men racing towards him. They had reached the maple tree in the front yard when he shouted, "What brings you two out in such a hurry this time of the evening?"

"We come with terrible news," said Mr. Keating.

Timothy explained Julianne had gone to the Suttons' cottage the day before but never returned. The old sheriff listened, a search plan already forming in his mind. He went into the cabin, gathered his duster, an oil lantern, and his rifle. He shut the door behind him, and then, without another word to the two men, he trotted to the barn to saddle his horse.

"Where are you going?" Timothy called as the sheriff climbed in the saddle.

"I'm aiming to go out looking for your daughter. I've half a mind where to start the search."

"Hold up. We're coming with you!" Timothy said, turning his horse.

Brine shook his head.

"That won't do. You're no horseman; you know that as well as I do, and you'll slow me down. I don't want to put more fear in your heart than I know you're feeling, but time is the only thing we have at this point and we're losing that fast. Julianne can't be the one to suffer from your lack of skill in the saddle. Go home and comfort your wife. Lord only knows how this is hurting her after losing one child. I'll be out to your place as soon as I know something."

Timothy watched the sheriff ride off and was tempted for a moment to ignore his advice and give chase. Who did that man think he was, calling him out for the way he rode? And with his daughter out there? Finally, Timothy had to admit the sheriff was right. He was no rider and his daughter needed someone who could cover any distance. He headed home, knowing he had nothing good to share with this wife.

"He didn't go after her?" Michael shouted without realizing it. "What kind of father just goes back home and sits on his butt while his little girl is missing?"

Grandmamma didn't answer for a long time. They looked at each other and something passed between them. Michael felt a voice in his head, "Not all fathers are bad, Michael. Sometimes there are reasons for what they do, even if we don't understand them."

"Timothy didn't have a choice, Michael. Remember that. It's very, very important that you remember that," Grandmamma said coldly, staring directly at Michael with a look he'd never seen before. "Remember that. Timothy didn't have a choice."

Brine knew the best place to start was the Sutton cottage to figure out which direction Julianne had walked. By the time he arrived at their home along the great tree line that bordered Donbridge, he approached cautiously. From a distance, he shouted to John Sutton to come to his front door. Finally a voice floated out the cottage window.

"What can I help you with, Jonathan?"

"The Taylor girl is missing, and this is the last place she was seen. I'm trying to figure out when she left."

Sarah came to the window and asked, "What do you mean she's missing?"

"She hasn't been seen since leaving her parents' house yesterday, Mrs. Sutton."

Sarah told the sheriff Julianne had left around nine, and Brine's heart dropped into his stomach. Far too much time had passed since the girl had struck out for home. He thanked the Suttons for their help and rode off in the direction they suggested.

A hollow orange glow from Brine's lantern lit up the path. Ahead of him, a mounded object lay frozen in the wood, bathed in the shadowy fringes of lantern light. He dismounted and approached the object cautiously, murmuring words of comfort to his jittery horse. He called in a cautious voice, hoping it was young Julianne, but only silence answered him. He had no choice but to creep to the pile.

The bright fall moon and the lantern's glow threw shadows around the woods, playing tricks on the old sheriff's eyes. Brine grabbed a stick and went to rustle the mound. A burly raccoon leapt from the mounded pile, hissed angrily and scurried into the woods, causing the horse to whinny and back up on its hind legs. Brine grabbed the reins tightly and brought the horse down, stroking its muzzle.

The sheriff felt foolish for letting the dark of night and the spook of the forest get the better of him. He was a lawman and had been for longer than he hadn't been. But tonight, with the shadows crawling around him and a young girl out there on borrowed time, he was afraid.

He chastised himself and pressed on. The temperature had dropped since the afternoon, causing the blanket of clouds overhead to drop snowflakes about the forest. Brine knotted the reins around his hand, bowed his head, and continued on foot, shielding his face from the blowing snow. The snow fell for some twenty minutes and then, as though the faucet of a sink turned off, it stopped. The clouds moved on past the fall moon, casting shadows on the ground as they drifted.

Brine walked for nearly two hours before his lantern reflected off a shale bank bordering one side of the road. On the outcrop of jagged stones, the ground was lightly covered in snow. As he rounded the corner, the sheriff came upon a shadowed spruce tree under which he saw a small body covered with leaves and snow. She was motionless and cold to the touch; Brine spoke to her, but his request went unanswered. The sheriff knelt beside her and lifted her to his horse; then he wrapped tight arms around her and smacked the reins. He rode off through the forest and cut through the tree line, making use of the Millers' alfalfa fields as a shortcut. The horse's mane fluttered in the night wind, and a long shadow enveloped the three of them as the bright moon lit their way.

Brine slowed his horse when he saw the faint orange lamplight shining through the doctor's front window.

He slid from his horse, pulled Julianne's body into his arms, and carried her to the porch. He rapped on the pine door only twice before a withered gray-haired man opened it ever so slightly. The doctor smiled with relief until Brine pushed his way inside, still holding the lifeless young girl.

"Is that... is that the Taylor girl? What happened?" the old man asked in a somber voice.

"Doctor Finch, I've brought fearsome news," Brine began. "Julianne never made it home from visiting the Suttons. I rode out from their place in the direction she took and found her where she'd fallen against the shale outcropping. Look here."

Brine laid Julianne on the doctor's dining table, one that had seen more broken bones set and stitches sewn than home-cooked meals. Dr. Finch had removed a swollen appendix on that table once or twice when it had been called for. But even the good doctor could not undo what God had already ordained. There was no bringing the dead back to life, at least not that night.

“What is it you aim for me to do, Sheriff?” the doctor asked slowly, his eyes growing moist at the sight of the little girl. He’d missed her birth for her coming so fast that the Sutton midwife had delivered her, and now, here in his dining room, he was acutely aware he’d missed her death by a matter of hours, too.

“There’s not much as can be done, I suppose. But after the way her mother took the news of losing her son, I just couldn’t bring her to their house. Not like this, anyway. I thought it best I bring her here, and then break the news to her parents. They’re already worried sick; showing up with her thrown across my saddle seemed wrong.”

"I understand, Brine," he responded, clapping a gnarled hand softly against the sheriff's shoulder. The doctor moved across the dining room to a chestnut breakfront and reached into the top drawer, drawing out a single white table cloth. He slowly draped it over Julianne's lifeless body. "If you'll be heading there now, I'll go after Mrs. Canfield. She'll be happy to wash the body and prepare her, but I don't aim for that woman to find out before the girl's parents."

"Aye, I'm headed that way right now. This isn't the kind of news that can wait 'til morning. Death and babies always come in the dark of night, my mama used to tell me. Thank you, doctor."

"It's no trouble at all. But do me a favor. The next time you need my help, please let it be for a cobbler that needs eating... not a young 'un that needs burying." His words would have sounded callous coming from any other man, but from the old man they were a plea. As a doctor to the village, he'd known great pain and heartache. Brine nodded and rode off to deliver the horrible news.

It was nearly sun up by the time he reached Timothy and Mary Ann. He followed the worn carriage path that wound around the Taylors' hayfield and led straight to the farmhouse. The cedar shakes were damp brown in the early morning light, and the remnants of ice and snow from the night before were nearly gone. As Brine slid from his saddle, the sun crested the Steerage Mountain range and morning dew glistened. The first birds of the day sang lightly over the trees, and yet the forest stayed dark on the outer edge, holding vigil over Julianne's passing. Brine was exhausted, but he knew he would need to carry himself better as he approached the Taylor house.

Mary Ann was waiting for him, passing the long hours rocking in her maple chair, watching for the sheriff to arrive. Her hair was tied haphazardly in a bun, a loose strand snaking its way across her face. Brine walked his horse over to the ring attached to a stable rail and tied him. He patted the horse briefly and murmured a soft word of thanks for the hard effort the animal had put in. As he ran his hand along the ridge above its velvety nose, he gathered the words in his mind to tell these folks about their daughter.

"She's dead, isn't she?" Mary Ann whispered in a hollow tone.

A chill ran down his back as he heard the haunting words. He climbed the steps of the porch and waited for Timothy, who abandoned his work in the vegetable garden, dropping his hoe on top of a row of plants.

“Well, did you find her? Where is she?” Timothy demanded, searching the sheriff’s face. Brine looked at his boots and nodded. He reached inside his duster and pulled out Julianne’s satchel, handing the empty bag to Mary Ann. Instead of taking the bag from him, she looked away. She sat as though in a trance, her eyes fixed on the cedar swing hanging still in the cold morning air.

In her mind, she saw Julianne, swinging and laughing, running around the yard. As she watched this vision, a grey hue washed over it and the yard returned to its former cold silence. The proof of an empty yard made the reality of the sheriff’s words sink in. She fell forward in her rocker and sobbed. Timothy rushed to her side and knelt down beside her while Brine felt he intruded on their agony.

“I’m so sorry, Timothy,” Brine began. “Let me hitch your horse for you so you two can ride to Dr. Finch's place. That's where... well, it's where I brought Julianne. If it's all right with you, I let him call Mrs. Canfield to help prepare her..."

"Thank you, Sheriff. That's kind. We'll just go on in and get ourselves ready while you do." Timothy helped his wife to her feet, slipping an arm around her waist when her knees buckled before she could take one step. Grief, a grief she'd been stabbed with before, made her weak.

They traveled silently along the road, winding through the field where the dark tree line cast a shadow over them. They stopped at the entrance to the forest, marked by two stone pillars on either side of the dirt road standing guard over the woods. The horses stamped their feet and whinnied softly as they tried to back up. But the three of them pressed on and urged the horses forward, slowly crossing the unseen line into the forest as a fog rose up from the leaves.

The deeper they went into the forest, the dimmer it became as the sunlight bled lightly through the canopy of leaves. Even the echoing chirps of far-off field birds faded away to silence. Further ahead, piercing the growing darkness, a condensed sunbeam broke through and pointed the way to a small corner of the forest, illuminating the doctor's cottage.

"Is he home, do you think?" Timothy asked in vain. There was still hope this was all a bad dream, that the doctor had managed to revive Julianne and was at that very moment riding off to tell them.

"I should think so. Look," Sheriff Brine answered, pointing. Smoke billowed from the stone chimney of the doctor's home, lessening the fog that surrounded them and filled the forest.

“Oh,” Timothy replied, crestfallen.

Overhead, blackbirds circled the cottage irreverently. The dark, unwelcoming sight and the smell of death and fear rushed over Timothy; he began to shiver. Mary Ann appeared unfazed by anything happening around her. She was in her own world, sitting beside her husband just as lifeless as her daughter must be. It was clear to Timothy his beloved wife was slipping away just as she had many years ago when their son had passed away. He could only hope she’d find her way back to him.

Timothy slowed the carriage and brought it close to the front steps. He climbed down from the seat and went to his wife to help her from the wagon. Mary Ann looked straight on at the cottage. As she moved up the stairs, the doctor came out and greeted them in the doorway, taking her hand gently. He was dressed in his usual white shirt and dark trousers, his clothes matching his somber mood. Brine decided it was best to stay outside.

As the Taylors walked through the entryway of the doctor's home toward the dining room, he pressed forward and approached the covered body of Julianne. Timothy and Mary Ann looked down on the sheet that covered the body of their only remaining child. A stream of tears fell over Timothy's face. He could not bear to look and turned his head slightly. Mary Ann watched as the doctor slowly removed the sheet. Beneath the cloth, Julianne's face was a solid white, her lips cobalt blue. Mary Ann gently touched Julianne's tiny hand and began crying deep tears. Timothy, a lump already formed in his throat, held back. He gathered enough strength to stand behind his wife and hold her close. The doctor left the room to join Brine on the porch.

"I've never seen anything like it, Sheriff," the doctor said in a tired voice as he took a seat across from Brine.

"What's to see? There was clearly a wound on her head. I'm sure if I went back into the forest, I'd find Julianne's blood on the rock. The child tripped and fell, probably skipping the way little ones are known to do. Didn't she fall and hit her head?"

"I'd have thought so, too, but it struck me as odd that a fall could be fatal. After all, if I don't have at least one fretful mother a day bringing me a babe who's fallen on his noggin, I would call it a boring day. Children fall, plain and simple. But they rarely die from it. Think of it this way, they're so close to the ground!"

"Then what are you saying?"

"I'm saying someone had to use enough force to propel the child forward hard to die from the impact."

"So you think someone pushed this little girl down hard enough to crack her head open, then... what? Just walked away?"

"Stranger things have happened," the doctor answered, looking out over the porch rail at the tree line that surrounded them. The fog had grown thicker, wrapping the house and its ghostly guest in a thick blanket of vapor. "Especially in this forest."

Both men were silent as they weighed the doctor's words. There was no reason to speak aloud the thought they carried in their hearts: there was a force at work in the forest no one could explain. Everyone in the village knew it, but no one spoke of it often.

Inside the house, Mary Ann pulled a chair next to her daughter and fell into it. She talked to her in a loving voice, whispering what sounded for all the world like a chant of some kind, watching her little girl's serene face. Timothy watched his wife, thinking of the time their son passed. He should take her from the room, but Mary Ann wouldn't leave, not for a long time. Her heart was dying with every chanted word, as though she was willing herself to go with Julianne's spirit.

When she finally rose, Mary Ann asked Timothy to leave her for a moment. He hesitated, fearful of what she might do, but then left the room and joined the men on the porch.

"I can't tell you how sorry I am, Tim," Dr. Finch began, but left the rest of his thought suspended in the cold air between them. His years of practice had taught him there were no words that could lessen the pain and therefore no sense in wasting them.

Timothy nodded, looking at the ground. “It hurts, I won’t lie. We’ve only just started to heal from losing the baby, and now to lose our girl, too... it’s not right. I should have driven her myself. I should have told her to stay at the Suttons ‘til I could come for her. If I hadn’t let her walk home, she’d never have been in the woods. She wouldn’t...” A single sob choked him, and both the sheriff and the doctor looked away as he unleashed his grief.

“You can’t do this to yourself, Timothy; it wasn’t your fault. It was...” The doctor caught himself, stopping in mid-sentence and changing course. “It wasn’t nobody’s fault. It’s just one of those things we don’t understand, for reasons we’ll never know.”

Sheriff Brine looked at the doctor sharply, but Timothy continued to look down, letting the tears fall. He had to be strong for her, stronger than he'd been when they lost their son. He'd blamed himself then, too, first for not thinking to fetch the doctor when something might have been done, and then for not seeing the pain that quickly drove her mad. Timothy loved Mary Ann, and he wouldn't let her suffering lead her to harm this time.

Mary Ann stood beside Julianne and her fingers itched ever so slightly. A silver ring, black with age and tarnish, rested on her right ring finger. The skin beneath it began to feel warm. As if it had awakened a memory, the ring continued to heat up as she raised her hand. The story of the ring came flooding back to her.

"Wait, is this another story?" Jasper asked, leaning his chin on his hands on the dinette table. "What happened to Julianne?"

"Didn't you hear me? Julianne died, sweetie. Remember? She hit her head?" Grandmamma said in a sad, kind voice.

"But she can't be! Why is her mom's ring acting funny?" Michael asked. Instead of kicking Michael under the table, Jasper waited patiently for Grandmamma's answer. She looked at the children and shrugged her shoulders.

"I don't know what to tell you, boys. I... well..."

"But her ring! Her ring has magic powers, right?" Michael cried. "Can't her ring bring Julianne back?"

"Oh, dearest. Mary Anne thought so, too, the poor woman... she remembered the story of the ring and of the mystery that surrounded it. For generations the ring had been passed along to the first born daughters of her family. Each woman who wore the ring developed extraordinary gifts."

As the story went, gypsies traveled the foothills of Donbridge and camped on the outer edge of the town near the great tree line each year. They brought side shows of wonder, animals from far off lands, and tiny shops of trinkets and treasures the likes of which the townspeople had never seen. The wagons with their massive wheels and sturdy hooped frames were amazing, strong enough to weather any storm and hold an entire family throughout their travels. These carriages were pulled by groups of donkeys or horses, strong animals that would pull the heavy wagons for thousands of miles around the country.

The gypsies always arrived at the beginning of summer and stayed only five nights. On the morning of the sixth day, their entire caravan vanished with no sign of wagon trails or any other trace of them. As all Donbridge folks have always known, the only way into or out of town was by way of the forest roads, but there was never any mark the gypsies had been there.

The morning of their arrival began with the gypsy caravan cresting the hilltop, their colorful wagons creating a hypnotic mirage that waved through the tree border. The town crier, Mr. Abilene, spied the group from the church's bell tower. As he did with most visitors who passed through, he climbed on his horse and rode out to welcome them to the town.

The coming of the gypsies generated a buzz through the town. At the Deep Barrel Saloon, men talked about the strangers' gambling tables and the card tournament that lasted for days before all the others were eliminated and a winner was declared. As for the women, they talked about the various clothing, the creative knick-knacks and sundries always charming to the eye. Children were thrilled the gypsies were in town because it was Friday, and Mrs. Davenport would allow them to leave school early that day. Many of them had saved their money for months to spend at the gypsy carnival or at the tiny shops which lined their campground.

Meredith, Julianne's great-grandmother, was a girl of no more than thirteen years at the time. She was conservative, not outspoken like her brothers, Lane or Fredrick. She was a silent dreamer, and she always kept her thoughts to herself. The gypsies' arrival each year only proved what she'd always known, that there was a world beckoning to her beyond the great tree line.

Standing on her family's front porch on the first night of the gypsies' arrival, Meredith looked out over the waters of Nelson's Pond and saw groups of people dancing and cheering near the large bonfire blazing in the middle of the carnival. Their sounds were far off echoes, but the joy was carried out over the valley. Soon the sounds of jingling bells, pithy lutes, and tinkling harpsichords began to drift high overhead. The sounds were enchanting and different from anything she had ever heard before. Feeling a bit foolish for keeping herself from the merriment, she climbed the slight hill toward the bonfire.

As she walked, she could barely make out the looming shadow of the Middle Tree, a large oak that had grown in the field for nearly four hundred years. As she passed the great oak, the vaporous glow from the far-off fire illuminated a strange carriage nearby. Sitting comfortably in a worn wooden chair was the

Phuri Dai of the caravan, known to all as Regina. The old woman's silver hair glowed white against the flames, and she wore a glazed look.

"Come closer, child," she said as Meredith peeked around the corner of the carriage.

As she approached the old woman, Meredith saw smoke rise from the woman's long straw pipe. Taking the pipe from her wrinkled lips, the woman asked, "What do you seek, girl?"

Meredith was bewildered; she had never been asked that question before. "I want to be special."

The woman sat in silence and took a long draw from her pipe. Then she asked, "Why do you feel you are not special?"

Meredith told the woman everything about herself, how she felt trapped in Donbridge, as though she couldn't breathe for the way the mountains around her held her tight. She told the old gypsy that most of her waking hours were spent in daydreams and her only wish was to see the world.

Regina listened quietly to the young girl, and then she laughed. “All of you children are the same, clinging to dreams of adventure and not wanting to wait for it to come to you.”

Meredith felt silly and out of place, as if she had poured her soul out for no reason. Just as she thought to turn around and walk away, the old woman began to speak.

“I have waited a long time for you. You are the one person with whom I can leave my gift. I lived these many years, decade after decade, contemplating my own life. And now I have finally understood my purpose… I was waiting for you.”

Regina stood and walked toward Meredith. She raised her hand and pulled a ring from her right index finger. At that moment, the fire in the distance rose high into the air. The people all around jumped back and shouted in fear. Regina held the ring up so it caught the firelight, causing it to glisten and twinkle like a strange rainbow, yet the ring was perfectly smooth.

"Hold out your hand," Regina whispered. Meredith was hesitant at first, but her heart longed for the ring, pulling her very center closer to the old woman. Meredith took the ring, amazed that it had no weight and was smooth to the touch. She placed it on her index finger and an odd sensation overcame her. Again, the flames from the fire rose high into the air until they touched the inky blackness far above, and then they settled as before.

"My dear child," Regina wheezed, "this ring was forged by my father many years ago from the days when the gypsies first began to roam the New World. He wrought it for my mother from a silver doll he found while digging for mushrooms, right here in this valley. My mother wore this ring for nearly two hundred years." She paused, waiting for Meredith to realize what she'd said, then continued. "As for me, I have worn it for almost one hundred sixty-five years. I am the last of my family's living elders. I have traveled the earth in this carriage and have seen the world at its worst and at its best. Never in my travels have I seen a place so beautiful, so quiet and touched with life, as this valley. But beware, darkness inhabits this valley, a darkness that only the strongest of protections can save you from. As for me, I have lived a long life, and now it's time for me to go."

Before Meredith could answer, her father walked up behind her and startled her. “Meredith, honey, what are doing here? Come to the carnival.”

As she turned around to thank the old woman, the carriage had disappeared.

“Where did she go?” Jasper demanded, pounding the table with his little fist. Michael sat transfixed, certain the explanation was coming. Grandmamma only smiled.

“Who knows? Where do all mysteries go when they are revealed?”

“What’s that supposed to mean?” Michael asked.

“Only this... you cannot ever know what you see, and you cannot trust what you hear. You can only believe in what you feel.”

Mary Ann, lost in memories of the ring’s story, plunged back to the reality of her daughter's death as thoughts of her grandmother Meredith faded. Julianne would have been the next to receive the ring, so she slowly pulled the tarnished band of silver from her finger. Just then, the oil lantern on the countertop began to shake, and the tiny flame in its burner rose high above its sooty glass chimney. But just as quickly as the flame rose, it extinguished, leaving only the light of day to shine into the room.

She placed the ring upon her little girl's finger, but no flames rose in the small cottage. The last tendrils of hope Mary Ann had clung to went out, even as a beam of light came through the window of the room and lit Julianne's cheek. For an instant, Mary Ann thought her daughter would suddenly take in a breath of air and awake, but that hope was gone as death held fast to her body. Just as quickly as the passing light came through the window, it vanished. The room went dim from shadow and the ring was dulled once more. Knowing it was now finished, Mary Ann kissed her daughter's cold cheek one last time and left the cottage.

When she stepped outside, Sheriff Brine had his hat in his hand and looked down. She went to the sheriff and the doctor each in turn and took their hands in hers.

"Strongest are the days that we press on, strongest is the will that drives us through the seasons, and strongest was the will of my daughter who is now with the ages. Know this, my dear friends, nothing happens in vain and dear Julianne did not die without meaning or prayer. She died in happiness, I can assure you of that. Weep not for those who have not been saved, but protect those of us you have saved.

By God, always remember to protect us mostly from ourselves."

Mary Ann climbed the carriage steps and placed a thick wool blanket over her lap. There was a look of sadness in her eyes, but there was also a firm sense of determination and will not even the heavens could shake. Timothy shook both of the men's hands and headed to the driver's seat. He placed his hand gently on Mary Ann's and held it for a moment. He slapped the horse's reins lightly, and the high wheels of carriage slowly began to turn until the couple traveled down the forest road.

Timothy was away in his thoughts, and Mary Ann began to nod off every few moments. Dreaming, she found herself at a river. The sky was crystal blue and light tufts of clouds burst open in a sunny sky. Embracing her dream, Mary Ann walked along the shore and saw a figure walking away from her. She didn't recognize it, but as she hurried closer, the image took on the shape of a giant wolf. The massive beast appeared to be heading toward a hill. Mary Ann followed it as fast as she could. She became so caught up in catching up to the wolf she never considered where she was.

"Wait! Wait for me!" she cried as the brambles in the tall grass pricked at her legs. A shoe came off in her haste, and she quickly kicked off the other shoe in her hurry.

She had to rest for a moment and leaned against a large stone tablet. She looked around at her surroundings and was frightened to find she was atop Starling Hill, the town cemetery. Stunned, Mary Ann looked about and saw a large hole in the frozen earth, ripped open next to two older plots. The wolf lay beside one of the headstones as if waiting for Mary Ann. Walking slowly through the maze of tombstones, she approached cautiously, watching the wolf for any sudden movement. The grey beast never moved. Mary Ann read the writing etched into the gravestone beside the wolf:

Meredith Masterson

A woman of unending nerve and life-light,
Hers is a light that will burn for eternity
Born February 18, 1640
Died January 7, 1785

Mary Ann was astonished at her great-grandmother's age when she passed. The numbers swirled in front of her eyes, refusing to hold still or make sense. In the same moment, she looked at the headstone to the left of Meredith's and saw her mother's headstone:

Molly Ann Howard

She sought life beyond life and
found joy in the process,
passing eternal hope to her family.
Born May 1, 1707
Died April 10, 1820

Could it possibly be that they had each lived over a hundred years? As she stood puzzling over this riddle, the great wolf suddenly stood and threw back its head, howling loudly over the hilltop. The shrill, hollow sound scared Mary Ann so much she awoke to find Timothy standing at her side of the carriage.

They were home.

Mary Ann slowly climbed down from the carriage and took her husband's outstretched hand. He held her arm as she walked to the front door of their house. Timothy helped her to bed. She was groggy and tired, and Timothy promised her a cup of tea to calm her once he was finished bringing the horse to the barn.

Soon, Mary Ann sat back against the pillows and watched the steaming tea as the tiny vapors rose above its rim and evaporated in thin air. She wanted to get up but had no strength left. She looked out the small window beside their bed and saw Mr. Teakwood, the undertaker, approaching in his wagon. He seemed to dance and swim as tears spilled from her eyes at the sight of the man who would see to her little girl's burial.

"Timothy, I am deeply sorry for your great loss. My services are at your disposal." Mr. Teakwood explained he would go to the doctor's cottage and retrieve the body of young Julianne. It was decided that a Sunday service followed by a burial atop Starling Hill would be best.

After all was planned, Timothy headed back to the house to check on his grieving wife. He climbed the porch steps but stopped short in front of the door. There on the porch, a red object lay against the door jamb. As Timothy got closer, he realized it was long stemmed rose, lying all alone and set perfectly along the door. Timothy picked it up and gently carried it inside.

Mary Ann had risen from bed and was busying herself at the fireplace when she turned and saw Timothy with the rose. She smiled, but then Timothy, honest man that he was, said, “It’s not from me.”

“Was there a note?” she asked, perplexed by its perfection.

“No note, and no clue where it came from,” Timothy said. He walked over to the kitchen counter and took a tin mug off the shelf, then dunked it in the water pail he’d drawn earlier that morning. He took a few sips, then set the cup on the wooden table and placed the rose in it. Mary Ann and Timothy said nothing more.

“Who gots flowers?” Mary demanded as she came into the kitchen, hoping for a cookie. “I love flowers.”

“Oh, just someone I once heard about,” Grandmamma answered in

an offhand way. "Never you mind about that, run along and let me finish dealing with your two brothers in here."

At the dreaded term "dealing with," Mary's eyes got big, but she did exactly as she was told. She skipped from the kitchen, happily clutching a cookie in each of her small fists.

"Whew, that was close! A story such as this one isn't fit for little ears, if you know what I mean," Grandmamma said in a hushed voice. Michael saw Jasper sit up straighter in his chair, proud to be counted among the ones who were actually old enough to be part of this kind of talk. "Now, where was I..."

As evening fell on that cold and dismal Saturday, Mr. Teakwood traveled back to the Taylors with Julianne's body inside his horse-drawn hearse. The sun had fallen below the mountain tops, and ahead where the forest was already firmly wrapped in the twilight, a shadowed figure waited on a large rock. Before the undertaker could raise his voice to ask who was there, it vanished into the woods without a sound. For a moment, the old man figured he'd truly seen nothing, but as he pressed on he began to feel less sure. He had heard rumors of a person living deep in the woods, but no one had ever seen this person or made any connections to who they were or what they were about. He had no choice but to try to put it from his mind as he pressed on.

As he turned into the main street of Donbridge, he saw Mr. Keating, his face covered in soot, fueling the lamps and beginning the work of lighting them for the evening. The lamplighter believed in making sure the lamps were spotless, and as such, every three days he cleaned the glass on each one. Mr. Teakwood found his red and white checkered handkerchief and held it out to Mr. Keating.

"My dear sir, you are in need of this more than I am at the moment."

The lamplighter laughed heartily at himself and said, "I must look quite a sight."

"Mr. Keating, I watched you clean the globes just yesterday. Were they dirty again so quickly?"

"Aye, it's the strangest thing. I had to scratch my head and wonder if I'd actually cleaned them or just dreamed that I had. It's good to know someone else was my witness. But this morning, as I made my rounds to put out the lights, the strangest feeling came over me. I felt my heartbeat slow inside my chest and my breath was hard to catch, and all of a sudden, the flames in every streetlamp burned white hot. They leapt so high they shot out of the tops. It burned brighter than the sun, I tell you! Then, just as sudden, they all blew themselves out, every last one of them. All that was left was soot, so much soot that every lamp was coal black."

Mr. Teakwood watched the old man's face as he explained, alarmed by the description of his heart failing in his chest but skeptical of the story about the rampant flames. He finally found he had no reason to doubt the old lamplighter other than the facts of science didn't line up.

"I see that you've retrieved little Miss Taylor, the poor dear," Mr. Keating said reverently.

"Yes, I have. She'll be buried beside her poor brother tomorrow."

"Don't it strike you as odd..." Mr. Keating began, but his voice trailed off, his words floating between them. He shook his head when the undertaker urged him to continue.

"No, you can't leave off like that and not tell a body what you're thinking! What were you going to say? What's odd?" Mr. Teakwood insisted.

"Well, I was going to say... don't it strike you as odd that we lose at least one child a year in this village?" The old man looked around, as though a culprit might at that moment be walking up behind him with evil intention.

"I don't see how that's odd." The undertaker, still clutching the reins of his hearse, bristled at the suggestion. "Death is a natural part of life. All life comes to an end at some time, and death arrives to claim its friend in different ages and stages."

"Yes, but when it's the children..." Mr. Keating looked around again before finishing his thought. "...when it's the little ones, they're not sick, they're not harmed, there's nothing wrong with them. They're healthy as your horse there one day, and the next, they're gone. Their bodies are just... empty."

"I don't think you've thought this through, sir," he answered hotly, uncomfortable with the turn the conversation had taken from someone who was usually so steadfast and dependable. “If you’ll remember, Julianne fell and struck her head. If the injury itself isn’t what brought about her death, then the fact that she bled out surely did. I think it’s best you stop listening to faerie stories and go about your job now. You to your business, and I to mine. To that end, I must leave your company to prepare the poor departed for burial.” Mr. Teakwood clicked his tongue for his horse to move on. Mr. Keating called out his thanks for the handkerchief and went back to his lanterns.

As Sunday morning dawned, a light fog shrouded the countryside. It rolled along the bogs of Masterson Swamp and stretched across the alfalfa fields. The day was only a hair warmer than usual and the remaining snow created a vapor against the morning air.

The church bell sounded the hour at seven o’clock. The town was still quiet, even though those with farms and animals to tend had been up for hours, all but Timothy and Mary Ann. They heard the bells ringing, but both were missing any strength of will to get up. Mary Ann finally slid from the covers and took her night coat from the hook next to her bed. She walked to the kitchen to make breakfast. She set the table with three plates and three cups, but as she went to get the silverware out of the drawer she stopped and began to shake. It was then she realized only two would be eating breakfast that morning and every morning from then on. She began to weep silently while Timothy watched her from across the room.

By noon, they were dressed and ready to head out to the Mass Reverend Connelly had prepared. Timothy went out to hitch up the horse. Just as Mary Ann was readying to leave, she saw her daughter's knitted scarf hanging next to the door. She took it down and held it tightly to her face. She could smell Julianne's scent, a combination of carefree happiness and the homemade soap Mary Ann scented with rose petals and lavender blossoms to overcome the strong smell of lye and ash. An image of Julianne's face formed in her mind as Timothy called to her from the yard. She stuffed the scarf in her dress pocket and headed for the wagon.

When they arrived at the church, the townsfolk watched them warily. A few close friends stepped forward and extended their hands to Timothy or took Mary Ann in their arms, but most kept a respectful distance, choosing instead to nod their condolences. No one said it, but the message was as clear as if it had been painted on the wall of the church: to lose one child was a sad thing, but to lose both of your children was the work of either God's wrath for some unrepentant deed or a dark curse placed upon the family. Either way, they wanted no part of it.

Never one to miss out on the opportunity to convince his congregation to repent and turn from their wicked ways, Reverend Connelly began the service with a reading from Scripture before launching into a sermon to put the great orators to shame. He held up Julianne as a shining example of one who'd had a pure heart and was at that very moment seated beside her Lord, promising those in attendance that the only way to ever meet again would be to ensure one's own salvation.

The church was silent when he closed with a final word of prayer. At some soundless signal, Mr. Keating, Sheriff Brine, Mr. Teakwood, Mr. Sutton, and Mr. Abilene carried Julianne's casket to the awaiting carriage. Mr. Teakwood closed the glass door of the hearse and drove the coffin up Starling Hill while the rest of the town walked behind. Timothy and Mary Ann walked apart from the group, staying to themselves in their misery.

The sun's rays slowly warmed the town as the overcast sky began to break up. Reverend Connelly waited patiently beside the grave, a hole whose size was a stark reminder this one was far too young to go. The pallbearers placed the casket at the side of the final resting place and then Reverend Connelly recited Psalm 23, words he had had to repeat at far too many graves, the repetition of which made him speak them from memory:

The Lord is my shepherd; I shall not want.
He maketh me to lie down in green pastures:
he leadeth me beside the still waters.
He restoreth my soul:
he leadeth me in the paths of righteousness for his name's sake.
Yea, though I walk through the valley of the shadow of death,
I will fear no evil: for thou art with me;
thy rod and thy staff they comfort me.
Thou preparest a table before me in the presence of mine enemies:
thou anointest my head with oil; my cup runneth over. Surely goodness and mercy shall follow me all the days of my life: and I will dwell in the house of the Lord forever.

The Taylors listened, grasping at the words of hope, and in their minds their daughter's life traveled at light speed. When the reverend was finished, the congregation filed past slowly to pay their respects and offer what words of comfort they could to Timothy and Mary Ann. A tall, thin boy approached and held his head low over Julianne's coffin, betrayed by a sudden tear that escaped his eye. Mary Ann finally recognized Samuel Sutton, and she smiled at the sight of the once rambunctious little sprat now taking on a more grown-up appearance. Julianne had often talked of Sam fondly, and the grieving mother was struck once again by all the things her daughter would never experience, such as a lost opportunity to have a sweetheart in this young man.

Soon, she realized they were alone with their daughter.

The two sat amongst the headstones for some time, not

speaking, not needing to. Off in the distance, deer gathered, grazing the fields. A sudden gust of cool air chilled them and with a whispered goodbye, they walked out of the Donbridge Cemetery's gates and headed home.

"But I thought..." Michael started to say but stopped when he heard his voice crack. He realized the last thing he wanted was Jasper calling him a baby. Michael cleared his throat. "But the ring, Grandmamma..."

"Yes?" she asked, getting up and going over to the stove to give the long-forgotten chili a stir. "What of it?"

"But... I don't get it. I thought if she had the ring she'd, you know, be immortal or something. She has the ring, and all the fires burned higher, and everything! What's gonna happen if they buried her and now she can't..." Michael stopped and looked at Jasper, who was watching his brother in terror-filled panic.

"Well, those things did happen, but they didn't happen in time, I suppose." She smiled that same sad smile she'd been wearing ever since she'd started talking. "You know, if this is too unhappy, I don't have to tell you the rest. We can go clean out some more of the trunks in the attic. You boys like that, don't you?"

Jasper nodded half-heartedly. They did like poking around in the attic of the old farmhouse, but today it didn't hold the appeal it usually did.

"You mean there's more? I thought once they—you know, buried her—that would be the end of it."

"Oh, no, Michael. There's no such thing as the end. There's always more to a story since the rest of the players move on."

Three weeks passed, and fall left Donbridge to be replaced by a more hateful season. The Steerage Mountains stood blue-gray against the cold winter sky. The trees were barren and the last leaves of the season were now scattered upon the ground. Mary Ann and Timothy had spent the last empty hours of fall canning and drying vegetables and herbs. In the smokehouse, Timothy had a swine he'd cured for winter storage. In the cellar, Mary Ann had filled her storehouse of vegetable boxes with carrots and potatoes, covering them in soil to protect the precious rations. Timothy had long since split logs into cords of firewood and stacked them evenly against the side of the house. The two had kept busy, trying not to let the darkness of their loss take up any room in their minds.

Mr. Tomley, the caretaker, had got a late start preparing the cemetery for the winter months due to the Taylor girl's recent funeral. The ground was inundated with frost as the cold temperatures froze what moisture was in the ground, meaning no shovel could break through it. In years past, he'd made a habit of digging a handful of spare graves before the first frost, lest anyone pass away during a hard freeze. With no time to prepare, anyone who perished during the winter would have to be kept until the thaw in the empty spare vault the town had commissioned in case of epidemic or plague.

Despite the work of preparing for the winter months, Mr. Tomley looked forward to November's arrival each year as it symbolized—in his mind, at least—the hard freeze months when the dead could no longer open their graves.

Of course, there were some who blamed the opened graves and the desecrated bodies on spirits or grave robbers, but old Tomley knew the truth: the dead were crawling from their graves, many of them getting so blinded by their sudden return to the land of the living that they got themselves hung up in trees or impaled on the wrought iron fence posts.

There were few who believed his theory that those caught in between living and dead were simply tired of staring at the lids of their own coffins and had devised a way out. Most folks blamed evil spirits or a strange ghostly visitor. In fact, Mrs. Sharp recalled hearing the spirits' triumphant howls echoing through the valley early one morning, just before dawn. On another occasion, Mr. Abilene swore he heard a clinking of chains and hideous laughter which made the hairs on the back of his neck stand straight up. Children in the town dared each other to wait by the gates to witness the spirits at their unholy work, but no one braved the feat for long.

No one had ever seen these spirits, of course, but the people were more than convinced they existed.

But one thing was for certain, it was Mr. Tomley who was tasked with the unpleasant job of freeing the poor deceased from where they'd got themselves hung up and stuffing them back in their boxes, adding more than a few extra nails for the ones who'd escaped their graves more than once. With November's arrival, Mr. Tomley sighed a breath of relief that the graves would remain quiet 'til spring.

Only the grave robbers knew the truth.

The evening stars dotted the cotton clouds as the moonlight cast shadows on the ground. A few yards beyond the cemetery, two men in ragged clothes with shovels perched across their shoulders staggered across the great field and headed toward Starling Hill. They laughed at each other's silliness and whispered in mocking tones about the people of the town.

As they crossed the field, the moon followed them like a spotlight in the night. They paused for a moment outside the gates and looked about. Then they worked their way between two of the iron bars they had long before bent to their size and sought out the freshest grave sites for looting. In a small fenced area, a large tombstone bore the name Brenner. One of the men slapped the other on the back and said, “Here lies a rich bastard.”

The other man laughed aloud, causing him to cough exhaustedly. Placing their shovels in the upraised mound of soil, they each began to dig. The dirt piled up quickly the deeper they went. As for the departed Mr. Richard Brenner, whose grave was in shambles at the moment, his spirit sat on an adjacent stone and watched the men in disgust.

The two dug at the grave site for nearly twenty minutes until sweat soaked their faces despite the cold night air. The dirt piled up outside the hole while the clinking of the shovels rang out above Starling Hill, as did their hideous laughter. Their shovels finally struck the coffin lid, which they greedily pried open. There, resting inside, Richard Brenner lay frozen in time with a pocket watch wrapped around his hands. It had been placed there by his wife, a keepsake from his grandfather, Nathan Brenner, who had planted the first orchard in Donbridge. Richard had loved the watch, and his enraged spirit rose from the tombstone and floated over to protect it from the men. His efforts were useless as the watch slipped through his hollow hands.

The older of the two men felt a cold shiver run down his back. "I think this watch is cursed," he said with a shiver. "You don't suppose... you don't think the Panderlaub put it in there to catch us, do you?"

"Now who's talkin' of scary tales? The Panderlaub's a myth, meant to frighten children into minding their lessons and doing their chores! We're scarier than the Panderlaub anyway!"

"Don't go making jokes about it. I saw the creature with my own eyes when I was young! He ate my brother's spirit while he slept in the bed!" The older man crossed his arms defiantly, daring his partner to argue.

"You're just running outta drink!" the other man said as he slapped him on the back and handed him a silver hip flask. The frightened man's hand shook, but he grabbed the drink and quickly sloshed back a few swigs of rum. His shaking stopped, and he grabbed the watch. His partner, in the meantime, had unbuckled Mr. Brenner's boots and began fitting them to his own feet.

"Not bad, huh?" he said as he showed off his newly acquired footwear.

As they finished gathering whatever else they could find of value, they turned Mr. Brenner upside down and placed the lid half off his coffin, leaving only his hand hanging out the side.

"Now these town folks will have something new to talk about. Maybe he got up out of his grave and fell over!" Mr. Brenner's spirit watched the men for a bit more and then floated off into the night as the two men moved on to another grave.

Next was Miss Prissy Sharp's burial site. The spinster woman had recently passed away of scarlet fever, but the men spied the fresh soil and began to dig it up. They had dug only about twelve inches into the ground when the going became more arduous. Her family, wanting to protect her from evil spirits, had mixed the grave cover with rocks and firewood to stop anyone from disturbing the dear woman's resting place. Their efforts had been sound for the men gave up and went to find another grave.

They found one whose tombstone read:

Julianne Taylor

Here lies our dearly beloved daughter.
May God bestow all his safety and care
unto her as we leave her to Him.
Daughter to Mary Ann and Timothy Taylor.
Born June 12, 1835
Died October 20, 1844

"Oh good, late October. Cold as it's been, this one shouldn't even smell yet!" said the younger man with a laugh.

"Have some respect, you dolt!" the older one replied. "We may be stealing, but there's no reason to laugh at their misfortune. Look at the tombstone; this one's but a child! She couldn't even own anything of value at her age. Let's just leave off with this one."

"What? Don't be getting soft on me now! Not after the respect we done showed by hanging half of them from the trees. Besides, a beloved daughter buried with nothing? Surely there's a silk blanket or a fine fur wrap inside, if not a pair of gold earrings or silver buckles upon her shoes!"

"Fine, have it yer own way. But still, be respectful of the dead, leastways when it's a wee one!"

The two men scattered the grave's dirt all about, creating a light dust in the air until once again their shovels slammed against the hollow sound of a wood coffin. This time a brief pause stopped their work; they felt as if they were being watched. Above and unseen, the spirits of Molly Ann Howard and Meredith Masterson hovered over their granddaughter's grave. Their haunting eyes stared in rage at the men desecrating Julianne's grave.

Throwing their shovels above the hole, the two made quick work of lifting the coffin out of the ground. The scruffier of the two grabbed his shovel and pried the nails loose around the edge of the lid while the other slid the top off the pine board coffin. Just as it came loose, the moon shown from among the clouds. There inside the casket, the gypsy ring's silver hue gleamed at the sudden beam of moonlight. Surprised by the light the ring created in the gloom of the cemetery, one of the men slowly reached for the girl's hand. He viciously began to pry the ring off her finger, but despite all of his efforts, the ring stayed put. Molly Ann and Meredith's spirits floated about the cemetery, crossing in and out of the tombstones. They even brushed the two men several times in an effort to ward them off, but they went unnoticed.

The second man laughed and said, "Give that hand to me, ya poor bastard, I'll get it off." He grabbed Julianne's hand, pulled out a buck knife, and began to cut her finger. At the same moment, Molly Ann and Meredith's spirits joined hands and descended over their granddaughter. Bowing their heads, their eyes began to glow fiercely as they glared at the thieves. The air above Julianne's body became thick with a bright, glowing white hue. The clouds in the sky froze as the man stopped cutting Julianne's finger. Not a sound was heard. A moment passed and then another. Suddenly, Julianne's eyes opened and the white light spread across Donbridge.

Panic grabbed hold of both men and neither had the courage to utter a word. Julianne raised herself from the coffin, gasping for air and gripping the sides of the wooden box. She yelled, and both men darted through the cemetery in terror, scrambling and fumbling through their hole in the gates. Julianne stood up, shaking, and watched the spirits of Molly Ann and Meredith approach, smiling. She didn't recognize either woman but felt a strange connection to them unlike any she had ever known. They each held out an airy hand to her then vanished into the cold night.

Julianne looked around and realized where she was. She could not remember much, but her head hurt terribly. She reached her fingers up to the side of her head and gently pushed at the angry wound there. She remembered hitting her head in the woods but had no recollection after that.

"They must have thought I was dead," she said to herself, but the notion was so odd she stopped thinking about it.

She walked out of the cemetery, but when she reached her parents' home she wasn't sure what to do. It seemed odd to walk in unannounced, so she knocked on the door and called out, "Mother! Father!"

Mary Ann, unable to sleep, had been in the kitchen, baking. A loaf pan filled with fresh pumpkin bread rested on the sideboard, its smell rising through the house. The pounding on the door woke Timothy, and the two looked at each other, surprised.

Timothy moved towards the door as another knock echoed in the room. Reaching for the handle of the massive door, Timothy paused and shouted, “Who’s there?”

“It’s me, Pa!” Julianne said.

Timothy quickly turned his head to Mary Ann, who had suddenly sprung forward from the oven. He slowly opened the door, and there, covered in soil and soaked in tears, was Julianne.

“Are we dreaming?” he asked as he reached out to touch his daughter’s hand. He smiled and pulled his daughter in for a hug. Mary Ann, who was still standing near the table, fainted and fell to the floor. Timothy rushed to her side to help her up. “It’s our daughter, Mary Ann! She’s back from the dead!”

“It worked…” Mary Ann whispered in an anxious, hopeful

voice. Timothy opened his mouth to ask her what she meant but shook his head. The woman looked to her daughter, holding out her arms toward the sparkling gleam of the ring on her daughter's finger.

"Thank you, Mother," Julianne said softly as she crossed the room and dropped down beside her. She hugged both of her parents, crying for joy. The three of them sat and cried their tears and laughed as their happiness took over.

"Mother, I am sorry about not getting you your herbs. Mrs. Sutton packed them in my satchel, and I had them with me. Did you find them?"

"Oh Julianne, do not worry yourself about such things. We never found them, but it's of no importance now. My daughter is home, and that is all that matters." Seeing that Julianne was filthy and in need of some care, Mary Ann got up from the floor and went to the linen cupboard.

"Mother, I really did have them and they were with me when I fell, but I just cannot remember."

"It's all right, Julianne," Mary Ann said as she handed her a towel and wash cloth. "Now wash up and prepare for bed, my sweet girl."

When Julianne had washed and put on a clean gown, her mother asked, "Ready for bed?"

"I am, and somehow, I am tired."

Mary Ann smiled and hugged her. "Good night, sweetheart. Sleep tight, but not too deep this time!"

Mary Ann tucked the covers around her daughter and blew out the candle. She joined Timothy in their bed and slept.

"That's it? She came home, and that's all? And they just acted like nothing happened?" Michael asked, sitting up straight.

"What would you have them do? Turn her out for being an evil

spirit? Their daughter was home, and they were too grateful to question anything," Grandmamma answered with a shrug, as though that explained everything.

"But what about all the people in the town? They knew she was dead!" Jasper argued.

"How did they know? They weren't doctors or healers."

"What? They went to her funeral! She'd been buried for weeks and weeks; of course she was dead!" he shot back. Michael could tell Jasper was getting mad, just like when they played a game and Michael would make him think he was winning and then suddenly beat him.

"Jasper's right; there's no way she could have survived. She was underground all that time, so she would have suffocated or dehydrated or starved to death..." Michael said, but he stopped speaking when he

saw the look on Grandmamma's face.

"Oh, I see. Well, it's just the story I was told. Maybe it's not true then," she said. She rose and went to stir the chili one last time. Jasper and Michael exchanged looks. They couldn't be sure whether her feelings were hurt.

They were saved from having to sit through her pained silence by Grandfather's appearance in the kitchen doorway.

"Okay, boys, it's finally letting up out there. If you'll bundle up nice and warm, I'll take you sledding at the hill above the old cemetery."

They forgot their chagrin as they yelled in excitement, racing off to gather winter things. Grandfather patted their heads as they ran past. Michael turned back to make sure Jasper hadn't left his cap on the kitchen table in time to see Grandfather cross the kitchen and take Grandmamma's hand in his. He kissed the silver ring on her forefinger and smiled.

"That chili sure does smell good, Jules. I bet it's warm enough to bring a body back from the dead."

Thank you for reading.

Look for Book 6

Fall 2017

To my fellow readers,

Please enjoy the recipes that follow. As the characters in the story enjoyed making them so will you be able to do the same. May they bring you closer to your family and friends and bring you joy for years to come.

All the best,

RD Vincent

Fall Harvest Pumpkin Bread

Batter:

3 cups of sugar

1 cup of shortening

2 2/3 cups of canned pumpkin

3 ½ cups of flour

4 eggs

2/3 cup of raisins

2 teaspoons of baking soda

1 teaspoon of cinnamon

1 ½ teaspoons of salt

2/3 cup of chopped pecans

½ teaspoon of crushed cloves

Directions:

1. Pre-heat oven to 350°
2. In a large bowl, combine sugar, eggs, & pumpkin
3. Fold in sifted flour and other dry ingredients
4. Mix in pecans and raisins
5. Lightly grease and flour a 9 x 5 inch bread pan
6. Bake for 40 minutes.
   Yield: 1 Loaf

Grandma's Old-Fashioned Blackberry Sour Milk Scones

Batter:

1 cup of sugar	2 eggs
4 ½ cups of flour	1 teaspoon of Van.
1 cup of shortening	1 teaspoon salt
3 tsps of bkg pwder	¾ cup of sour Mlk**

1 cup of fresh blackberries

Directions:

1. Pre-heat oven to 350 °
2. In a large bowl, combine shortening and sugar
3. Add eggs and vanilla
4. Sift dry ingredients and combine with batter, adding in the sour almond milk. Stir well
5. Refrigerate for 30 minutes before baking
6. Lightly grease and flour a baking sheet
7. Spoon the dough onto the cookie sheet, about 12 scones per sheet or as desired
8. Bake for 12 minutes or until edges are light brown.

   Note: The recipe can yield up to 25 scones. If so desired, the dough can be frozen for later baking.

**To sour the milk, add a tablespoon of balsamic vinegar to the Milk and let it sit for 15 minutes before using.

Northern Three-Bean Chili

1 pound of ground beef	1 medium onion
1 quart of crushed Tom.	1 large bell pepper
1 cup of kidney beans	½ teaspoon of salt
1 cup of pork and beans	1 cup blk beans
1 tablespoon Brn Sgr	½ tspn chili pwder
1 tbsp of peanut butter	½ tspn blk pepper
½ tsp of onion powder	½ tsp garlic pwder

Directions:

Dice the onion. In a small sauce pan, add ground beef, chopped onion, onion powder, salt, black pepper, garlic powder, and chili powder. Cook until browned, then set aside. In a small sauce pan, cook chopped bell pepper in water until pepper slices are soft. Drain, then add to the browned beef and onions. In a large pot, combine beans, crushed tomatoes, brown sugar, peanut butter, and beef. Simmer for 1 hour. Spice to taste.

About the Author

RD Vincent is an American author born in the historic village of Goshen, New York, on February 14, 1979. He was raised on a small dairy farm along with his brother and sister and attended Pine Bush Central Schools.

In late 1997, he attended SUNY Potsdam and began his studies as a Music Major. Feeling a bit overwhelmed in the music world, he sought refuge in both the English and Business Econ Departments. By the fall of 1998, he had a rare opportunity to meet New York author and poet Maurice Kenny. Over the next year, Vincent studied with Kenny in his creative writing class. Later that year, inspired by Kenny, he began writing for *The Racquette*, SUNY Potsdam College's Newspaper with a small cooking column called "Something to Cook About." The columns were published once every two weeks and contained a short story which always had the characters cooking or baking. Vincent included the recipes. It was at this moment that the idea for Donbridge came about while collaborating with his Grandmother and Great Aunt who both had a multitude of stories passed along to them from their elders. This project would take Vincent nearly 15 years to storyboard. RD Vincent's first publication, *Donbridge, The Ring of Lazarus,* was published July 15th 2015 on Amazon eBooks. This is the first of six novellas in the Donbridge collection.

DONBRIDGE
THE WITCH OF TAMARACK HILL
BY RD VINCENT

DONBRIDGE
The Miracles of Midwife Sutton
BY RD VINCENT

DONBRIDGE
The Hermit of Mapes Ravine
BY RD VINCENT

DONBRIDGE
The Lost Princess of Lenape Valley
BY RD VINCENT

R. D. Vincent